A Normal PIG

By K-Fai Steele

BALZER + BRAY

An Imprint of HarperCollins*Publishers*

Dialogue translations:

page 24, left to right: *Yes!* (Icelandic); *Shall we start by getting coffee?*
(Icelandic); *Do you have a map of the show?* (French); *But is it a picture
or a sculpture?* (Russian)

page 25, top to bottom: *These heights make me need to pee!* (Japanese); *Wow,
it's huge in here!* (German); *Let's see where the tour begins.* (Spanish);
Is there a senior citizen discount? (Chinese); *Someone told me we should start
on the top floor.* (Persian)

Balzer + Bray is an imprint of HarperCollins Publishers.

A Normal Pig
Copyright © 2019 by K-Fai Steele
For information address HarperCollins Children's Books, a division of HarperCollins Publishers,
195 Broadway, New York, NY 10007.
www.harpercollinschildrens.com

Library of Congress Control Number: 2018942265
ISBN 978-0-06-274857-7

The artist used watercolors and ink to create the illustrations for this book.
Typography by Dana Fritts
19 20 21 22 23   SCP   10 9 8 7 6 5 4 3 2 1
❖
First Edition

For K-Yun and K-Lone

Pip was a normal pig who did normal stuff.

She liked making art,

cooking with her family,

and thinking about what she
wanted to be when she grew up.

Then one day, a new pig came to school.

Pip didn't know how to respond.
It was just her normal lunch.

The new pig was in Pip's art class, too.

Pip hadn't changed, but she started to feel different.

When her parents asked her
what was wrong, she replied,

On Saturday, Pip's mother had an idea.
"Why don't we take a trip to the city as
a family?"

Pip had never been there before.

Pip heard so many different languages.

At the playground, all the pigs looked so different.

Even the food was different.

"Is there anything on the menu
that's not so weird?"

"Maybe it's weird for you,
but not for me. I like it."

When they got home, Pip was feeling better.

On Monday, Pip sat at her usual
table in the cafeteria.

"Maybe it's weird for you, but not for
me. I *like* my lunch. . . . Want to try it?"

And weirdly enough, by recess
Pip felt pretty normal again.